Anne-Marie was born and brought up in the Cathedral City of Salisbury in Wiltshire. Her dear father was a musician and from an early age Anne-Marie loved music and often sang in her father's band. Her mother taught her how to appreciate the written word and how to compose poetry. This love of writing never diminished and, therefore, once commitments allowed, her first book was conceived.

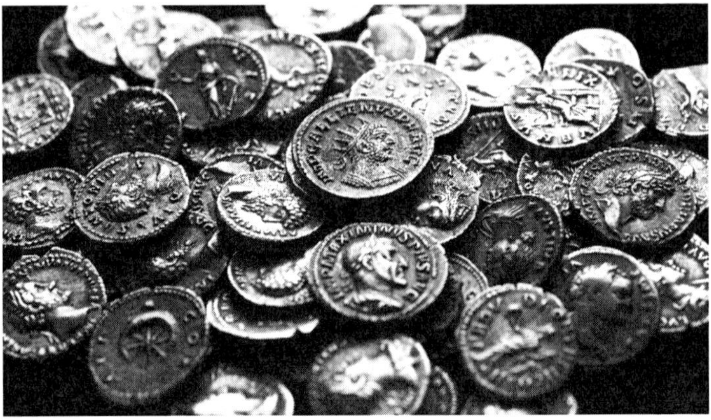

I would like to dedicate this, my first book, to my darling mother and father.
I have drawn on my own memories of early family days and also from their colourful recollections, which were often fondly discussed.

Anne-Marie Sassoli

GO BACK FOR LOVE

AUSTIN MACAULEY PUBLISHERS™
LONDON · CAMBRIDGE · NEW YORK · SHARJAH

Copyright © Anne-Marie Sassoli (2019)

The right of Anne-Marie Sassoli to be identified as author of this work has been asserted by her in accordance with section 77 and 78 of the Copyright, Designs and Patents Act 1988.

All rights reserved. No part of this publication may be reproduced, stored in a retrieval system, or transmitted in any form or by any means, electronic, mechanical, photocopying, recording, or otherwise, without the prior permission of the publishers.

Any person who commits any unauthorised act in relation to this publication may be liable to criminal prosecution and civil claims for damages.

A CIP catalogue record for this title is available from the British Library.

ISBN 9781528920247 (Paperback)
ISBN 9781528920254 (Hardback)
ISBN 9781528963039 (Epub e-book)

www.austinmacauley.com

First Published (2019)
Austin Macauley Publishers Ltd
25 Canada Square
Canary Wharf
London
E14 5LQ

I would also like to thank my dear friends for putting up with my endless questions and even writing some of the book whilst travelling by bus on a shopping trip!

I do hope you enjoy reading this story and hope you will look out for my next offering…
A murder, no less!

Anne-Marie Sassoli

Laura is left a very strange legacy by a distant Aunt whom she just barely remembers from her childhood. Wheels are set in motion when she opens her legacy to go back in time and trace her aunt's life—from adored rich girl to a destitute servant for her husband's relations and her drug addict son. However, things improve eventually and through forces that are unexplainable and maybe even extra-terrestrial, Bessy sets in motion an amazing time travel experience for Laura but will this have deadly consequences and what will happen if time is tampered with?

GO BACK FOR LOVE

Chapter 1
The Legacy

Laura opened her eyes and stretched her arms above her head, yawning at the same time; work again this morning, why couldn't it be Friday? It was freezing cold too, the bedsit she lived in was always cold, the old boiler (not the landlady) was just too decrepit to cope and was pretty pathetic at best. You could not even warm your hands on it as it was, perhaps, colder than body temperature and was like living in the arctic! It wasn't a bad little place to stay and fairly modern, really, but there was no double glazing, and all the heat disappeared through the old-fashioned windows which did not close properly. When it was windy, you could see the little curtains moving gently from the air pushing through. Oh well, if she did everything at a run, there was no time to get too cold, in theory! There was nothing else for it but to bundle quickly to the bathroom, take a very quick shower (a bath could wait till tonight), clean her teeth vigorously and pull on something half decent for work. Laura liked to think about what to wear on a daily basis and did not know what it might be until it was time to get ready. Now, this morning was cold and frosty so black, slim-fit trousers, a peach blouse topped with a black and peach jumper. Hmm... sounded peachy! *Just a little pun there thrown in for light relief*, she thought to herself, smiling broadly.

Black ankle boots, her black, soft, quilted coat, warm scarf and hat. That felt like a good plan and it was all washed, ironed and ready to wear. She liked it when a plan came together, another broad smile crossed her lovely face and she was off and running, literally, but not before she had grabbed the letter from the mat and hurried out of the door, still munching a rather burnt piece of toast between her teeth, as she shut and locked the door securely behind her. Humming to herself, she jauntily walked down the street, pushing the toast firmly into her pretty mouth to munch happily whilst humming and dusting her hands of crumbs as she went!

At least the library where she worked was pleasantly warm after the frosty walk by the park, where the children were running and playing already. They ran at full pelt up and down the green, stamping their feet and laughing loudly. It would be nice to do that today, just hop on a swing and fritter the day away with not a care in the world. However, she had to get to work where it was down to business and hushed whispers.

Laura felt in her pocket and pulled out the letter she had received this morning from a firm of solicitors. Weird, as she did not know any solicitors and had no reason to deal with any, not being in the position to buy a house or arrange her affairs, as she had absolutely nothing to arrange at present. She would save it until coffee time and have a proper look at it then. Meanwhile,

"Hello Mrs Ward and how are you today? What would you like me to look up for you on the computer?"

Her job was particularly satisfying in that, most of the time, she was able to answer her customers' queries and steer them in the right direction of a book they were looking for or just help them look up the right information to help with a certain task. It was interesting and never dull, just the opposite to what most people believed her job to be.

Yes, it was a little dusty and sometimes utterly frustrating when she could not easily help locate the exact book but also brilliant when the end product was found, and a very happy person left clutching their prize!

Yes, a completely satisfying job all round for someone like herself who enjoyed helping people and who loved her literature. Replacing *Wuthering Heights*, one of her favourite reads of all time, into its rightful place on the shelf, she glanced at the clock; it was time for her coffee break and it was most welcome.

Whew, what a long morning, although the customers were mostly really lovely and always chatted (a little quietly though) as they all liked to come to the library for a whole host of things; the most important of which was company and, of course, a warm place to stay for a while. It was a place where people could meet and quietly exchange the week's happenings with their friends whilst looking for a good read or a reference book. Laura cradled her coffee cup in both hands and luxuriated in the warmth felt through her hands, then sniffed slowly the pungent aroma before sipping the smooth milky contents.

Aha! Her letter. Putting the cup down, she reached for the letter, turning it over this way and that, trying to get a clue as to its contents (it was more fun this way), then making the decision, she inserted her thumb along the top fold to tear it gently open. Peering into the envelope, Laura extricated the pieces of paper from inside.

Very formal, Miss Laura Deborah Donahue… Laura skipped over the first few sentences until she got to the interesting bit…

Bequeathed by her aunt, Mrs Bessimer Blythe, her entire collection of coins, to be

handled lovingly and wisely, but, with a little caution!

There was a lot of very formal jargon; and to which, and to whom, and to what, but in essence, she had been left a collection of coins by an aunt she had probably only seen once or twice when she was very young. As her parents had split up and since her father had died, Laura had not had much contact with her family at all.

She was an only child who was not really wanted or cared for much and when she was of age, flew the nest as quickly as possible. Her mother had remarried and moved to France with her husband, not wanting to have any baggage to slow her down! Keeping in touch with family was of a very low priority to her mother and especially keeping in touch with her daughter. As far back as she could remember, her mother had only been interested in having a good time and going out, whilst Laura had been palmed off with a string of 'sitters'. Usually it was the next-door neighbour, who was a good woman and was extremely kind but equally, she was quite old and, it had to be said, was very set in her ways.

Laura was put to bed by 7 o'clock whilst Mrs McHugh watched the television, mostly the game shows with a cup of tea and biscuits. Therefore, Laura got used to being on her own and amusing herself as best she could. This explained her love of books and she would read avidly as the books led her into different worlds where she could lose herself in exotic places, be a heroin or find endless love.

This was, of course, executed by way of a torch under the covers, so as not to alert Mrs McHugh when she checked on her.

This, in its turn, increased her overall education, as a lot of the books she read were beyond her years but not beyond her understanding. She was a very wise young woman and this, ultimately, enabled her to secure a well-paid position working in a field she adored. Laura could not think of any other job she would like better really, as it ticked all the boxes for her own personal, professional career. Laura adored books as they had the ability to transport you to amazing places, tell a story whether spooky or serious or amusing. If you could read a book, you were never alone, and Laura had needed not to be alone in her miserable life.

So how strange this Aunt should think of her and send her a coin collection of all things. Had she showed any interest when she was little? She could remember sitting at a table with many coins spread around and a very elegant lady, with immaculate hair and wearing velvet gloves, tapping them and regaling lots of happenings and events connected with them. Her recollection was very hazy but she remembered her aunt's lovely smile and soft-spoken voice. She also remembered that her aunt was a very attractive lady and her hair was platinum white, which seemed to shimmer as she moved her regal head.

It was quite amazing really, someone had left HER something.

Laura was really excited about this turn of events and had a million butterflies in her stomach and almost as many in her head. At last something was happening, even if only on a small scale, it was enough to send a small ripple through her uneventfully calm life so far. Now, where and when was she to go and pick up this collection?

Laura thumbed through a telephone book and found the solicitors, who had an office in town. She would go and ask Mary, the senior librarian, if she could have some time off soon to enable her to visit their offices and find out more about the legacy.

She had a million thoughts skimming through her quick mind and a small fission of excitement zinged through her as to all the possibilities awaiting her.

'Rotherby, Smythe and Dorrington', said the gold plaque on the wall. Well, here she was, might as well see what exactly her aunt had left. Opening the black, shiny door with a brass handle, she walked up the dark stairs to the first floor. Laura sniffed the air which was slightly stale and dusty, just what you would expect of a solicitor's office, she supposed. At the top of the stairs, almost opposite, was a door marked 'Reception'. 'Please Enter', which Laura did, cautiously opening the door that actually led to a light and airy, fairly modern office. There was a young girl sitting at the front desk and she lifted a bright, smiley face to Laura and enquired as to whom she had come to see today. Upon consultation of her letter clutched in her left hand, she asked for the gentleman who had written her the letter and was told to take a seat whilst he was contacted. Laura did not have to wait long and was ushered into a room off to the right of reception.

"And so, my dear, Mrs Smythe remembered that you listened very intently to her reminiscences and loved to hear about the coins and where she had acquired them— so here you are," the very portly gentleman pushed a large envelope towards her with gusto, puffing slightly with exertion. "I am sure you will look after them wisely. Oh and what I did not explain in my letter is that a small legacy also comes to you in the sum of £20,000, to do with as you wish."

At this point in time, Laura was thoroughly bemused and then to be told she had been left £20,000 was just unreal. She had never had much money all her life and lived up to her income most months. Her mother had never given her a brass farthing and said she had to make her own way in the world and she had, even though now her mother was quite a wealthy woman. However, Laura was content that it was that way and had never asked or wanted anything from her, although, in her heart, she would have liked a loving arm to have been folded around her at times when she was young and had been feeling sad or lost.

The man her mother had gone to France with was very wealthy and he had a thriving business with several properties, none of which Laura had ever seen or been invited to. He had been married previously and had a son and a daughter from that marriage. They were absolutely spoiled rotten and had made it pretty clear from the outset that they wanted nothing to do with her. Laura shrugged her elegant shoulders and raised her eyebrows, accepting their decision, keeping her distance at all times.

Yes, she had a few hundred pounds tucked away, just in case, but that was about it. Twenty thousand pounds, was this really happening to her, really? Yes, it was fantastic and thank you very much Aunt Bessimer-Blythe, thank you very, very much.

The appointment concluded with much handshaking, nodding and smiling. Eventually though, Laura found herself out onto the street, walking slowly along the pavement, reading the contents of the will letter slowly. Why on earth had her aunt left her the collection of coins and why the legacy, however, she was extremely grateful that she had. She remembered her aunt had handled the coins very carefully whilst wearing her velvet gloves and had told Laura not to touch them.

Laura hugged the letter to her and looked at the key she had been given to a safe deposit box at the Bank, all very proper and also extremely exciting. All she knew was that she could move out of the little bedsit and she might even be able to buy her own small flat, now that she had some sort of a deposit and money to sustain her for a few months. Excitement welled up inside her. She could never have envisaged such good fortune. Putting an extra spurt on, she made her way to the bank which was in the High Street, if she hurried, she might get there before they closed…

"Yes, madam and what can we do for you?" said a very smartly dressed young man at the information desk.

Laura explained her purpose and was immediately asked to wait while Mr Germain Atkins was called down to see her. Laura looked about her as she sat waiting and observed the continuous stream of customers entering the bank to pay bills, deposit cheques and money and withdraw funds from their account. Maybe she could now become one of these affluent people with her new-found fortune. Within about 10 minutes, a tall, dark, smiling gentleman came towards her with his hand outstretched in greeting. Laura stood up and shook hands with Mr Atkins and was shown into a small office at the back of the bank. Mr Atkins had to unlock the door and then lock it (he explained that it was procedure), then motioned for her to sit opposite him at the large desk. Laura settled herself down, folded her hands in her lap and waited.

Germain Atkins peered at Laura as he put down a large metal box he had taken into the room. This girl looked so tiny and fragile but held her back very straight, looking at him with her pretty blue eyes. Her hair was worn in a long bob to her shoulders and was sleek and shiny and it swayed gently when she turned her head.

Her heart-shaped face was devoid of make-up, except for a little lip-gloss on her full lips. "Aa… Hum," said Mr Atkins, "this is quite straightforward, do you have the letter from the solicitors?"

Laura handed over the signed letter and on perusing it, Mr Atkins pushed the box towards her.

"I think you will find you are the owner of a very fine collection of coins. They are not worth a King's ransom but would probably fetch a fair amount if you were to auction them."

Laura raised her face towards him and smiled serenely, "I don't think I will sell them, at least not straight away, I want to look them over and just handle them, like my aunt did, as I know she found pleasure in doing so."

"I am also intrigued as to why she left them to me as I cannot really remember her very well, I was so small when we met."

Mr Atkins shook his head slowly from side to side and made a shrugging gesture with his palms upwards.

"I am afraid I am as much in the dark as you are my dear as I did not personally deal with your aunt, but you must have made a big impression on her to have left you the tidy legacy and the unusual coin collection."

"Try not to dwell on it too much and enjoy your gift, you are young and hopefully it will stand you in good stead for your future."

Laura smiled again at this really very kind man and stood up, offering her hand in a parting gesture, but then decided to go on tiptoe and place a light kiss on his plump cheek. This flustered him a little but he was so pleased by her warm gesture that he too smiled broadly.

The meeting was concluded fairly speedily then, Laura picked up her box and was given her letter back, said farewell to Mr Atkins (who said he would help her with any financial affairs should she wish in the future) and she was again out on the pavement in the centre of town.

Chapter 2
Go Back

Laura made her way home deep in contemplation, let herself into her little bedsit, put on the kettle for a cup of tea, shrugged off her coat and curled herself up on the little sofa. When the kettle boiled, she made a strong, hot cup of tea and carried it back to the sofa where she sipped its refreshingly warming contents gratefully. Much later, when she had finished her tea, she opened the box and peered inside. There seemed to be quite a large collection of old coins but what fascinated her, lying on a bed of velvet, were several pouches. She pulled open the first one and placed her hand inside to pull out a coin and…Whoosh… it was like a force whistling past her, her skin felt clammy and the air was cold. She should have put on the little electric fire… no, it was more than that… wherever was she? Laura looked around for all the familiar things she was used to, but they had faded into a mist-like distance – still there but beyond her reach.

I must be tired, she thought, *and pretty emotional, maybe I need some sleep to recharge my batteries.*

However, as she went to get up, a strange feeling took hold of her and she looked down at her hand where she was holding a coin between her thumb and first two fingers, the date was so clear – 1927.

Laura then looked up and she was no longer in her flat but somewhere quite different with huge windows, richly decorated walls, beautifully covered chairs and the sun was flooding into the room like a golden stream.

Laura's heart was beating like a drum and she could feel the perspiration beading on her forehead but at the same time she felt cold and clammy. What was happening to her and why? The room was now totally in focus and Laura sat up, then she jumped and let out a small cry, for sitting opposite her on a red velvet chair was a little girl who was watching her intently with her head on one side, obviously waiting for Laura to speak.

"Who are you?" the little girl asked, "I am sure there was no one in here before and I have only been to get a drink from the kitchen.

"Are you the new maid?

"You don't look like a maid.

"What funny clothes you are wearing!"

Laura did not know what to say as the same questions were going around in her own head. The little girl had the most beautiful hair, cascading down over her shoulders, it was tied with a ribbon at the top. The ribbon matched her lovely dress, obviously made of silk and she had on high button boots. "Come on Laura, don't be stupid," she told herself, "you have fallen asleep and you are dreaming, now wake up, this is not like you at all, to have daydreams or whatever this was," it really did feel quite weird and she shivered involuntarily.

"I'm Laura," she heard herself saying, "Who are you?"

The little girl stood up and approached her, "I am Bessy of course," she said, with much attitude. "I know who I am but I am not so sure about you."

"You look a little strange and you have a sort of strange light around you.

"Are you from around here?

"Have you come a long way to see us?"

Before Laura could answer the questions, Bessy was talking again.

"Do you want to come and play with me in the garden before tea, we would be allowed."

The little girl put her head on one side and waited for an answer, summing Laura up as a possible playmate.

Laura knuckled her eyes and pushed her hands up onto her cheeks as if this would clear her vision and her head, what on earth was going on? It seemed as though she had gone back in time and (this was a crazy notion but would not go away) was now conversing with Aunt Bessimer when she was a little girl. *No, this is crazy, what on earth am I thinking, I have drifted off to sleep and this is all a dream.* Laura picked up a sizeable amount of flesh on her arm between her fingers and pinched HARD! Ouch! That jolly well hurt, and she rubbed her arm vigorously to alleviate the pain.

"What did you do that for?" said the little girl, moving forwards from the window.

"Are you alright?

"You seem very pale, I could ring for the maid to bring some water for you if you like?" She moved closer to Laura and tried to put her little arm around her shoulders as if to comfort her but could not reach Laura somehow.

Laura lifted her head and smiled at the little girl, "I am fine, just being silly but I think I might be lost as I did not mean to arrive here.

"You say you are Bessy, would that be short for Bessimer by any chance?"

Nodding, Bessy pulled a face and scrunched up her little nose, "Yes it is, but I hate it, so Bessy is fine, and I only answer to that anyway. Can you come and play now 'cos everyone is out, and I am the only one here, I hate being on my own, although I make up lots of stories and read books and things, but it's not the same as having someone to play with."

Bessy put out her hand and Laura went to clasp her own around it, but then Laura dropped the coin she had been holding and immediately, as though on total rewind, she had a strange, empty sensation and a feeling of being drawn through space at terrific speed, there was a ringing in her ears which was very uncomfortable if not pretty painful and she covered her ears with her hands to try and ease the discomfort, losing track of time and space in the process. It seemed as if she was in some sort of tunnel with a kaleidoscope of colours swirling around her, almost akin to riding a helter skelter but without the safety of the walls. Suddenly, everything stopped, there seemed to be a weird vacuum where her ears felt blocked and her head filled with cotton wool. It was as if she were floating through space with no noise and total blackness then… thump, she arrived with a heavy bump, in her own bedsit, sprawled on the floor of the hall near the front door.

Laura looked around her and examined her hands, which felt cold and were shaking. Slowly, she pulled herself to her feet and gingerly felt herself all over as she felt quite bruised and battered. What on earth was all that about and how did it happen? Had she fallen asleep and had a really vivid dream? Never had she remembered any of her dreams as clearly as this one though.

It had definitely been a long day and Laura had a splitting headache so she rummaged through her handbag for some painkillers and swallowed them with some water from the kitchen. That was about as much as she could handle at the moment and, stumbling a little as she walked, just about managed to get to the sofa, curled herself in a little ball, gently laid her aching head on the cushions and drifted into a deep sleep.

A few days had gone by since the afternoon of the 'strange occurrence', and Laura had gone over it again and again but could not make head nor tail of it all, in fact, it had completely baffled her logical thought processes and so, wisely, she had put it out of her mind for the time being, to be mulled over again at some later date.

On waking from her sleep, she had put her box of coins away and rung a few friends to tell them of her good fortune, promising to meet up with her best friend for a coffee and chat to tell her all about the plans she had for her future. Maybe, just maybe, life was on the up for her and for the first time in her life, she could see some sort of future opening up before her.

Now that Laura had some funds, she had been telephoning estate agents for particulars of small flats in the area and had even been to see one or two. There was one property in particular she liked and it was just nearby. An old house had been made into two flats and had been very sympathetically modernised without ruining the beauty of the building. Flats were leasehold but this one, as it had been recently renovated, carried a longer than average term.

It was in her price range and after putting down her deposit, would still leave her with some savings for a holiday maybe and a little nest egg for a rainy day. Things would be very tight for a while but it would be worth it to own her own property.

Time had gone by and Laura had been in her flat for about three months. She absolutely adored it and had got settled in very quickly. So far, she had not seen much of her neighbour but it was not a problem as she had been so busy moving in and choosing new furniture, carpets and curtains that she was too exhausted to be sociable at the moment. As she understood it, the whole property belonged to the person who owned the much larger flat and to whom she paid her yearly maintenance.

This suited Laura as it meant she did not have to worry about the outside garden but could just enjoy it.

It came with a parking space to the side of the property and, if she so wanted, she could use the washing line discretely positioned at the back. Everything was just right for her particular needs and her single status at this moment in time. Laura secretly hugged herself as she could never have imagined owning anything in her lifetime, especially this really attractive property, and it was all hers. Yes!

Still sleepy and partially wet from her shower, Laura went to the front door to retrieve her letters, she yawned delicately and began shuffling through them with speed, as mostly they were 'junk' and promptly ended up for recycling.

Hello, this was an unusual one, it had a very distinctive emblem on the top and looked very official.

Laura hooked her thumb under the flap and opened the letter deftly, extracting the letter from within.

It was from a firm of coin collectors and somehow, they had been informed that Laura had a coin collection, and would she like it valued? Um, would she, she had not really given it much thought over the last few months and after the first experience had been reluctant to look at them again but she supposed she should give it another go, surely it had been that she was tired and had fallen asleep? Laura thought about it all day at work and when she arrived home that afternoon, had her usual, long soak to take away the stresses of the day and then made herself a small dinner, today it was going to be spaghetti with her own pasta sauce, which was quick and easy, she made herself a mug of tea, unearthed the coin box and sat down at her little table in the corner of the living room.

Laura scrutinised the box as she munched her way through her meal and thought about her last experience, surely it was just a dream as she had been really tired.

When she had finished her meal and sipped her hot tea, she pushed her plate to one side and drew the box towards her.

It felt like Pandora's box and she wondered if she should open it but telling herself she was being silly, she lifted the lid and peered in.

This time she chose another velvet pouch and pulled on the strings, she put her hand in and pulled out another coin, this one had the year 1943 clearly visible through the grime and once again she felt that truly extraordinary feeling as if an icy blast had claimed her and pushed her bodily through the air, the wind rushing by her face was so severe she scrunched up her eyes to stop them stinging. Her ears were hurting again and she covered them, trying to minimise the sound. The feeling of spinning was really strong this time and she wondered if she would ever right herself. There was no way she could open her eyes against this fierce onslaught so she kept them tightly shut to alleviate the sickness she was starting to experience. Dramatically, after this incredibly windy, noisy journey, she was deposited with a dull thud on the floor of an all-white room, which smelled faintly of ether and disinfectant.

She scrambled to her feet and tried to perch on a chair in the corner of what looked like a hospital room but she could not sit, as the chair had no substance, so she just seemed to hover there.

The room was very old-fashioned with a metal bed in a sort of pale green colour, the only other piece of furniture. A woman was sitting on a chair by the bed, leaning over with her head in her hands, sobbing wildly. There was a figure in the bed, but it was still, and Laura guessed this was not good.

"Why, oh why, did you have to leave me Arthur, what am I going to do? I have the baby and just enough money to pay the rent for another week. How did this happen, I can't believe you have left me. You promised me everything, and how we were going to live a life of luxury, it never happened, did it? You did try and recover your losses after the business failed, but it was never the thriving business you led everyone to believe. I ran away for you and gave everything up, they said you were too old for me, but I didn't care. Now I have a baby boy, but how am I going to care for him, what is to become of us?" The woman dissolved into tears again.

A door opened in the corner of the room and a nurse came in, dressed all in white with a white nurse's cap, sporting a huge bow at the back.

"Come along now Mrs Blythe, you must not upset yourself so, Mr Blythe was in a lot of pain and I am afraid there was nothing we could do to save him."

The nurse went over to the woman, who lifted her head, and it was then our eyes met and she seemed to recognise me as an incredulous look came over her face. The nurse looked in my direction too but did not seem to see me as she looked at the woman and gave her a hug, urging her away from the bedside and out of the door.

They disappeared and Laura knew who the woman was, Mrs Blythe, Mrs Bessimer Blythe, she had somehow caught up with Aunt Bessimer again, only this time in 1943, and she must have married the man lying in the hospital bed and had a baby and now he had died and she was destitute. I know she recognised me, I know she did, thought Laura, as of course, she had not changed but Aunt Bessie had grown into a woman. She was also sure the nurse did not see her. Somehow, Laura had been whisked through time and space to arrive at the year on the coin she had handled. Laura looked down at her hand and knew that if she let go of the coin, she would, in all probability, go back to her sitting room.

Could she help Aunt Bessimer at this time or would events unfold irrespective of her presence, Laura wondered. She did not like it here in the hospital room and also did not like to be a witness to the event that had just happened but it was so, and she could not change it.

Quickly, Laura let the coin drop into her pocket and, instantly, she felt that push against her body and a rushing noise in her ears. She quickly curled her body up, holding her hands over her bursting ears and knew she was being carried back in time to her own flat. As before, the journey was very bumpy and the idle thought came to her that this is what Alice felt like when she disappeared down the rabbit hole.

That thought was instantly followed by fear and she began to shiver, her teeth chattering violently, her body being tossed from side to side.

Chapter 3
The Meeting

Uuumph... She felt winded and there was a ringing numbness to her ears and they hurt. As before, she put her hands up to cup the sides of her head and just let the dizziness subside. Laura started to take note of her surroundings and found she was in a half-sitting position on a carpeted floor. She looked up and realised she was actually outside her flat this time, curled up, right next to her door, but OUTSIDE. *I do not have my keys with me,* was her first thought as she lay there, partially dazed and winded from her incredible journey...

"Hello," came a very deep voice to the back of her, "are you OK there?"

"Have you had a fall or something, here, I'll help you up."

With that, a strong pair of male arms clasped her from behind and under her arms, gently assisting Laura to her feet. Laura turned around on reaching an upright stance and found herself loosely, but firmly, held to a very broad male chest. She let her lashes sweep upwards and met the most entrancingly blue eyes she had ever seen, in fact, they actually gave her a little shock-like feeling and she shivered involuntarily.

"Hey, are you cold?

"You are shivering so.

"How long have you been there?

"Is this your flat?"

The questions came too thick and fast for Laura to process at first and she just continued to hold her gaze on the stranger's enquiring blue eyes.

"I am so sorry I have not met you before but I have been away.

"If you give me your key, I can let you in." Again, poor Laura felt there were too many questions and too much information wanted, Laura could not cope at the moment.

"Um err… No, I'm quite alright, just a little dizzy but OK," she reassured as she saw him widen his eyes in alarm.

"Yes, this is my flat but I have locked myself out and have not got the key."

Laura tried to remove herself deftly from his strong grasp, although it felt really quite good. The man, realising he was still holding her, slowly took his arms away from around her body and waited while she steadied herself.

"OK," he said, "you seem better now but you still seem very cold, don't worry, I have a master set of keys in my flat. I actually own the building but decided to make it into two flats as I was not making use of its full potential, I occupy the larger flat. If you can just wait here, I will nip and retrieve them, I hasten to add, they are only for emergency use and I was meaning to introduce myself to you but I have been away on business and, what with one thing and another, just haven't got round to it yet."

He spread his hands towards her and asked,

"You OK to wait there a minute?"

Laura nodded and gave him a weak smile, whereupon he raced off up the corridor.

Laura leaned against the wall and shook her head in an effort to clear her mind.

What a bizarre set of events and what a strange way to meet your neighbour who was extremely good looking and also very tall, well over six foot. He was rather well dressed, sporting a dark grey suit and a crisp white shirt and silk tie.

He was her leaseholder, then? No ordinary neighbour this one, maybe, he was a lawyer or an accountant, something BIG in the city no doubt.

Before Laura could properly take stock he was rushing up to her brandishing a large set of keys. He quickly tried several before he came upon the one that opened her door and deftly threw it open, standing back for her to go past him and into the hall.

Laura entered her flat, and it was just as she had left it, however long ago that had been. She glanced at her watch, only about 10 minutes, probably the time it had taken to meet her new neighbour and for him to get the keys. How weird, she had not been gone long at all but felt that she had been away for hours. Forgetting herself, she turned back towards the man and apologised for the inconvenience she had caused and thanked him for his prompt help. He followed her into her sunny lounge, looking round and taking in the neat, prettily decorated, uncluttered room. Laura had good taste and had chosen beautiful, calming cream and coffee tones, with a large modern rug taking centre stage.

"I'm so sorry, I don't know your name," said the man. "Mine's Blair," and with that, he strode towards her, extending his hand.

Laura took his outstretched hand and shook it. His handshake was firm and true, and he looked straight into Laura's eyes with his own twinkling blue ones.

"And your name is…?" he pushed his chin slightly forward and looked expectantly at her.

"Oh, I am so sorry, it is Laura, I seem to have completely forgotten my manners. Please do sit down," she gestured to the comfy modern sofa covered in a soft, suede fabric.

"Would you like a cup of coffee?"

Blair sat down on the sofa, hitching his trousers up at the knees.

"Yes, that would be lovely Laura, it has been a long morning, however, I can only stay a short while as I have several appointments this afternoon." Laura made her way into her bright, modern kitchen. She had fallen in love with it on sight.

It was just the right size with everything to hand and the units were made of a light-coloured wood with the worktops finished in a light marble effect. It always looked so warm and bright and she loved working in it. Quickly, she looked for the coffee pot, then went to pull two coffee cups from the cupboards. Turning her head slightly, Laura shouted, "How do you like your coffee?"

The reply was so close it made her jump as Blair was standing just feet away, observing her, as she stretched up to the cupboard on tiptoe, lifting one leg as if to get more height.

"Here, let me," he said, easily reaching past her and taking two cups and two saucers from the cupboard, he placed them on the worktop. Watching him, Laura realised she had not moved and was still half-poised at the open top cupboard.

Pulling herself together, she got motivated and bustled about getting the sugar and filling the percolator with ground coffee beans, then reached into another cupboard for some biscuits, really crunchy caramelised ones that went especially well with aromatic coffee.

The kitchen felt too small as Blair leaned nonchalantly against the worktop, just watching her as she went about her tasks, with a slightly amused air.

"So, Laura, what were you doing on the floor outside your room without your key?" Blair asked, folding his arms, looking at her in consternation, as if suddenly, it didn't add up.

Laura, busied herself with the cups and kept making the coffee, sniffing the pungent aroma emanating from the coffee cups as she poured the hot nectar into them. Laura thought quickly.

"Oh, umm I thought I heard a noise at the door and as I was in the middle of something, quickly opened it and looked out. I had forgotten I had wet hands and stepped out of the doorway to see if someone was walking down the corridor. When I turned back, the door was just about to slam shut so I turned tail and ran to stop it. As my hands were wet, I lost my grip of the door handle and somehow ended up on the floor, in a heap, the door firmly shut."

Whew, that sounded pretty good actually.

Laura had finished the coffee, not turning to look at Blair, deftly arranging the cups, sugar and cream on a tray, before picking it up, ready to take it through to the lounge. Quickly, Blair pushed away from the worktop and took the tray out of her hands to carry it for her to the coffee table at the side of the sofa.

"Bet you won't do that again in a hurry, huh?" he said and smiled.

Laura smiled back and nodded.

Twenty minutes later, Blair was taking his leave of her; they had had a chat and caught up on when Laura had purchased the flat and how it was possible (leaving out the coins bit) and he had explained how he thought it made sense to make the large rambling house into one large flat and a smaller one, as he was not there a lot of the time. This would mean there would be someone in the building at all times and his flat did not need the upkeep the whole house had needed. He said he was glad he had met her at long last and at which point, Laura had blushed and looked down at her hands and he said he hoped they could catch up again soon.

When Laura closed the door, after Blair had left, she slowly walked across the room in deep contemplation at what had happened. She now firmly believed that she was going back in time somehow and seeing a window of her aunt's life through the medium of the coins. Did her aunt know this would happen, is that why she left them to her? What could she do, what purpose did it serve?

So many questions going round in her mind, Laura walked into the kitchen and started to make her evening meal, not really concentrating on what she was doing. The easiest meal was a salad, so she gathered the ham, lettuce, tomatoes and potato together and started to assemble them all on a plate. When she had finished, she carried it on a tray into the living room, with her freshly made tea and ate slowly, turning everything over in her mind but making no logical conclusions that made any sense. Sometime later, she washed up her dishes and made her way to bed, too tired to stay up thinking about it anymore.

Several weeks had gone by and Laura had been working hard at the library. The hours were long, although she did get a decent salary. The coins had occupied her thoughts more and more and she had decided that tonight, she would try again and see if it was a mere coincidence or something more extraordinary was going on. She had seen Blair on two occasions, both times not for long, either leaving the building and seeing him drive off with a wave of his hand, or just as he was about to enter his flat, in which case, he did not even see her.

On the second occasion, Laura had admired Blair's tall, lithe figure, as he disappeared through his door. He was really handsome, but it was no good thinking along those lines, as men like Blair did not look twice at someone like her. How Laura had obtained this negative opinion of herself was hard to see, as she had the most beautiful chestnut-coloured glossy hair, worn in an edgy bob. She had a heart-shaped-face with large, dark eyes; her lips were full and soft, slightly protruding, and therefore, a little provocative, had she but known it.

The trouble was, Laura was very shy and had little self-confidence. This was due, in part, to her mother Grace, who had no time for her and always told her she was useless at everything; the way she dressed, what she did, how she did it. Whatever Laura did, it was never good enough and she tried so hard to live up to her mother's expectations. If only she had been given more encouragement and support when she was young, goodness knows what she could have become. It was a relief when her mother went to France and left her to her own devices, as she had gained more confidence on her own.

However, men were an unknown quantity really, she had dated a little, and one boy had been quite special, but they were more mates than boyfriend and girlfriend and he had gone abroad to work for two years. They still kept in touch, but he had met someone on his travels and more often than not would extol her virtues non-stop so that Laura had backed off, giving him the space he so obviously needed. She had several girlfriends and one special friend but did not go out much as she preferred to spend her evenings in her little flat as by the time she got home and had tea, it was at least 8 o'clock, which left little time in the week for partying.

She did meet Lucy occasionally, however, mostly on a Saturday, and they would go shopping and have a coffee. Then they would go out to the theatre or a film in the evening, finishing with a glass of wine, but that was not often. The trouble was, neither of them had much money and everything was so expensive. It has been a while since they had last gone out together, so maybe, she would contact her to see if she fancied getting together, mainly for a chat to catch up on events and mutual friends. She was bored just staying in every night and after everything that had happened, wanted to share her current news regarding her legacy.

OK… Laura was ready to try again and had gone into her bedroom, the furthest room from the front door (whether that would make a difference, she did not know) but for added insurance, she made sure she had the front door key with her, safely tucked away in her pocket. Now to try another coin. Laura pulled out another little black pouch and as before, grasped the coin which she slowly pulled out.

As it came into view, she saw the year 1955 and as she was trying to turn the coin in her fingers, that strange sensation took a hold and she was spiralling down and around until her whole body shook with the sheer force of it. This time her body actually shuddered and shook and she could feel her teeth snapping together. First she was cold then she felt hot, so hot, it was like being in a furnace. On and on she spiralled, until it all stopped as suddenly as it had begun and she seemed to drop into a black void. When she opened her eyes this time, she was in some sort of a yard with cobbled stones.

Carefully, Laura rubbed her arms as they felt sore and she had several bruises. That was some journey! She picked herself up and looked around, there was a really pungent smell, sort of smoky and fishy at the same time, very odd!

In one corner there was a tin bath filled with what looked like shellfish of some sort and over to her right there was a metal boiler, which had steam emanating from it, with yes, she was sure, crabs' claws waving around. How utterly bizarre! Wherever was she? Laura walked down to the back of the yard and there were several doors, one of which was open and on peering in, there were rows of fish on spears, with a charcoal like substance on the floor. It was smouldering and the smell was overpowering, making her cough and splutter, quickly backing out of the door.

A smokehouse, surely. She had seen pictures of such places when she was looking through some of the books describing life in the 50s in the library. It is amazing what information you picked up and then retained for use at a later date! This was a fish curing yard, preparing shellfish and fish for sale. It was very gloomy and grubby looking, as though everything needed a good scrub. I suppose where the fish were smoked and cured, it just permeated everything.

As Laura turned round, she saw Bessy descending some steps from the house into the yard followed by a tall, well-built woman, who was carefully made up and had auburn-coloured hair which must have been very long as it was plaited and wound around the top of her head. From her scarlet daubed lips hung a lit cigarette, which was at complete odds with her elegant hair and face, she began shouting at Bessy.

"What do you mean you have not had time to wash the shellfish, I certainly have not got the time and they need to be ready for sale tomorrow. They need to be thoroughly clean, ready for sale, get the bamboo rod and agitate the tin bath up and down until you see the water muddy, then that needs to be emptied and fresh water fed in through the hosepipe, you know the drill by now, so get a move on. Need I remind you that you were given a roof over your head and a home for that sickly son of yours, now hurry up and get them washed and ready to go."

With that the large lady disappeared into the house, stomping up the steps, muttering as she went, the cigarette still hanging from her lips, smoke emanating from it to spiral thinly up into the air.

"Good-for-nothing girl, waster of a son, why we took them in I do not know."

Bessy was bending low over the large bath containing the shellfish and swishing them around with a large rod as she had been instructed to do. It looked hard work and she wiped her hand across her forehead several times. To one side, there were wooden boxes with sieve-like bottoms, stacked up and with a large scoop, Bessy was ladling the shellfish into the boxes, stacking them up, one on the other. She must have sensed someone was watching and she turned quickly, meeting Laura's eyes.

Comprehension dawned and once again Bessy recognised her. Gone now was the confident little girl and the pretty woman. Bessy looked miserable and forlorn, very thin and her hands were red raw.

"Look at me, look what has become of me, I have to work for the family in their business in order to survive and bring up my son. They treat me like dirt and all I am is a lacky," her head lowered onto her chest and she heaved a huge sigh.

"Everything smells foul and I am bending over from morning to night, my back feels like it will break if I have to do another day. They took me in as a kindness, they say, but no one would work for the pittance I get and the attic room is cold and draughty and my son is always ill with colds and coughs. Hopefully, I will spend more time in the shop as at least, I meet people and have a chat now and again. Can you believe it has come to this?"

She started sobbing, great, gulping sobs, which were absolutely heart-wrenching. Laura went to try and comfort her but found she could not cross to where she was and could only get within about 3 to 4 feet of her before there seemed to be a barrier in front of her. Laura went this way and that but there did not seem to be a way through. *Could she hear her,* she wondered?

"Bessy, can you hear me? What can I do for you? I don't like to see you like this."

Bessy looked at me, the tears drying on her face.

"Yes, I can hear you and sort of see you, but you are like an image in the water, with no real substance. I thought I had been seeing things, you came when I was little, didn't you and again when I lost my husband, I remember you.

"You have such a kind lovely face.

"Where do you come from?

"Are you a ghost?

"If you are, I am not afraid as you seem to calm me and this living hell I am in does not seem so bad when I see you, as though there will be a time when I will be happy and free."

"Do you know, can you tell me? I need to get away. Can you help me?"

She held out her hands in a beseeching gesture and Laura tried desperately to reach them but could not breach the unseen shield.

"Hang on in there Bessy," she cried.

"I will try and help but I don't know how, I am sure things will get better, you have got to believe in yourself. You are such a lovely woman and have been so strong. Hold your head up high and fight for your right to a decent life for yourself and your son.

"Oh, Bessy, can you hear me?"

It seemed to Laura that, try as she might, the time line or whatever had brought her to this point in time had closed and she was left in a vacuum, moving further and further away from Bessy, who she was sure could not hear her and now probably could not see her.

Laura looked at Bessy and her heart went out to her, how could she help, she could not break through the barrier, only her voice carried.

"Bessy, I have visited you before I do not know how it happens but you have left me some coins and I can travel through time, picking up your life at intervals, the only trouble is, I do not know how to help you as I cannot reach you, maybe it is true that no one can change time and therefore it is not possible."

Laura felt the odd kick in her stomach and knew she was on her way back, somehow, she had let the coin fall out of her grasp and immediately, she was whisked back through time, with the familiar ringing in her ears and the cold had once again taken hold of her and she spiralled downwards, ever downwards, picking up speed as she went. This time she just seemed to fly through the air, strange patterns swooshing past her, flame-like tongues reaching out to pull her onwards. Time, space, whatever this was, it was like nothing she had ever experienced before and her body felt charged with a huge energy, so great that she wondered if she could bear it.

Thud!

She was unceremoniously deposited, this time, in the hall just inside her front door, and therefore did not need the added insurance of her key!

Laura felt devoid of feeling and all her energy had been sapped by that last trip.

She dragged herself up from the floor and made her way to the sofa in the lounge, where she gingerly sat, her head cradled in her hands, just getting her status quo back.

Why could she not help Bessy?

Why was she able to go back in time?

What was behind it all, the purpose, if of course, there was one?

Poor Bessy, how awful to be trapped in a life she hated and so different from the one she was born into.

There must be an explanation somewhere but at the moment she was too tired and curling her feet up on the sofa, she promptly fell asleep.

Laura could hear the phone ringing and hurried from the kitchen to answer it. "Hello, Laura speaking, how can I help?"

"You can help me polish off a bottle of wine and a bowl of chilli tonight, if that is possible?"

Laura looked at the mouthpiece of the phone and wondered if she had heard correctly.

"I am sorry, could you repeat that, I think you have the wrong number."

There was a deep chuckle on the other end of the line and the same rich voice said, "No, I am sure this is the right number."

"This is Blair here and I was wondering if you would like to come to my flat for a bite to eat tonight?

"I have been so busy working and have only caught glimpses of you as I have been hurrying out so thought we could get together for a catch-up chat, that is, if it would be OK with you?"

Laura was totally caught off-balance by Blair. This really fit, good looking man was asking her out for a meal.

Wow and double wow, but, should she go? A little voice in her head said, "Take charge of the situation Laura and go for it." Her heart was thumping and a little pulse was ticking in her temple.

"Um, I… don't know, what time would that be?"

"Any time that suits you, say about 7:30 or 08:00? I don't bite, you know."

At this last comment, Laura chuckled deep in her throat in an excited sort of way and just said (to her amazement and surprise), "Yes, that would be lovely, I'll see you at 7:30 then, bye."

"Fantastic! OK see you then," said Blair and put the phone down.

Laura was left staring at the phone in her hand as if it had a life of its own.

"What have you done my girl, what are you going to wear?"

She could feel the goose bumps on her arms and wrapped them around herself, she was excited and pleased, glad she had said yes, but oh, so scared. She had this feeling that somehow, meeting Blair was just inevitable and somehow meant to be, it felt right somehow and although a frisson of excitement coursed through her at the forthcoming evening, it felt good.

"Now, not much time to get ready, shower, what shall I wear? Oh no! Formal, informal, skirt, casual trousers," as Laura was racing to the bathroom, her mind a whirl for the time being, the coins and Bessy had taken second place but had not been forgotten.

"Hi, come on in and take a pew," said Blair, with a flourish as he opened the door to his flat wide for her to enter. Laura sort of dipped down under his arm, which was holding the door and scuttled past him.

"Just keep going straight and you can't go wrong," said Blair, as he finished shutting the door.

Laura, did as she was told and entered a delightful room, very tastefully furnished, slightly masculine, but not too much, the wall lights casting a warm glow over everything. Laura hovered by an occasional chair and Blair came up behind her and moved her over to the comfy sofa, finished in a burgundy leather which was, oh so soft and oh so expensive! It felt lovely when she sank down into it and let her mind go blank.

She had spent so much time choosing an outfit, discarding others on the bed, on the floor or hung up around her bedroom, that she was late and flustered. Blair was asking her if she would like a drink and somehow she said, "Yes!" and chose a medium white wine.

The evening progressed very pleasantly; Blair was an excellent cook and host. He kept up a light banter of unusual stories about himself and mishaps at work which made her laugh. She felt really at ease with him and found herself telling him a little of her background and how she came to be here.

He was a little more reticent, not telling her too much about himself, other than that he had had a good education and gone on to university where he studied law. He was now an established lawyer with his own progressive business, which apparently took all his waking hours to run. He was obviously passionate about his work and it showed in the animated way he described some of the different facets of his working day. He was extremely well known and often took on cases for clients abroad, taking him away for weeks at a time. He was rather sad as he had lost someone dear to him recently, it was whilst he was away from home, but he did not go into details. It was at the point, when he said his own mother had abandoned him and he had been brought up by a very dear lady that little prickles shivered down her spine.

He said his father was left to bring him up as best he could and he had met her, fallen in love and spent the rest of his life adoring her. His father had died several years before, and she had been left alone. A very independent woman, she had stayed in her own house for as long as she could and then, had a flat in a large complex adapted for the elderly, as she did not want to be a burden on anyone. This is how he came to be left the house and had decided to make it into flats.

Somewhere in her deep subconscious, Laura thought it was the house where she had visited Bessy, it was all very hazy, but could it have been why she was drawn to the house when looking for a property to buy? A shudder went through her.

They had finished their meal and were sitting at the table with their coffees when Laura raised her head and looked at Blair, as if seeing him for the first time.

"Can you tell me her name?" Blair looked up and met her eyes.

"Yes, of course, it was Bessy, although I called her Bess, both short for Bessimer, which she hated."

Laura dropped the spoon she had idly been stirring her coffee with and looked at Blair, wide-eyed.

"Did you say Bessy?"

"Yes," came the response and Blair looked at her expectantly. "Oh my word, it couldn't be, could it?"

"Was her name Blythe by any chance?" asked Laura.

Blair sat up straight now and looked at her keenly.

"Yes, yes it was, how the devil do you know that, have you met her? She never mentioned anyone."

"In fact, she did not talk about her family and friends at all, just said I was her only family and did not need friends."

"I thought it a little strange, as she was so personable and talked easily with people, but she never had anyone close and only made acquaintances."

This was such a revelation that Laura did not know where to begin. What did she say to him, "I am Bessy's niece and I am trying to piece together her life?"

Obviously, Bessy had met Blair's father and they had lived together, bringing him up, so Bessy did have a rosier future then, but how long had she had to endure her horrible life and where was her own son?

So much was going through her mind and there were so many questions. She sighed and then took a deep breath. She looked at Blair and said, "I don't know how this has happened, or why, but Bessy was my Aunt. I only remember seeing her when I was very little but not since, until I was summoned to some solicitors, as she had left me a small legacy and a coin collection."

Blair sat back in his chair with his elbows resting on the arms, putting his hands up to form a 'V' shape and just stared. You could see he was totally perplexed and bewildered by what she had just imparted and could not take it in no more than she could.

"But how has this come about, I dealt with all of Bessy's affairs and wound up the will, I knew nothing of a small legacy and any coin collection."

He shook his head from side to side and then rested his chin on his hands.

"You must admit this is a lot to take in, she must have put your little legacy in the hands of someone else and just not told me, but I don't understand why."

"I would not have stopped her, I have made enough not to want for anything and would not have minded."

"This clears up such a mystery you know, I have felt from the moment I met you that I knew you and that we were meant to meet somehow."

Laura gasped audibly and put her hand to her mouth. "I also knew it deep down that there was something, some tangible force between us and that we just had to make a connection at some time in our lives."

There, she had said it and felt that it was so.

Slowly, oh, so slowly, Blair got to his feet and came over to her. He lifted her up in his arms and she just seemed to melt against him. He had such a lovely sweater on, it was so soft and at first, he simply held her against him, wrapped her securely in his arms and hugged her. He then tipped her little face towards him and softly took possession of her soft, pliant lips which seemed to blossom under this deft touch. Lara felt an electric connection right down to the tips of her toes and her soft breasts strained against the little white blouse she was wearing. She wanted to savour this moment forever, she had never felt quite like this before.

A lovely, floating sensation took a hold and at the same time a fire was building from her core, threatening to engulf her completely in its flames. Blair increased the pressure on her lips and pressed even closer, so close she could feel him against her thin skirt, and although it should have alarmed her, it just felt so right and she welcomed him to her. She could faintly detect the delightful scent of his aftershave and luxuriated in the feel of his strong arms. If this was heaven, then so be it, she would stay right here.

All too soon, Blair raised his head and put a little distance between them.

"I'm so sorry Laura, I did not mean for that to happen, I did not mean to alarm you," and he stepped back from her, holding her shoulders in his outstretched arms.

"I'll take you down to your flat now, shall I, it has been an eventful evening in one way or another."

Laura felt as though she had been drenched in cold water, what on earth was she playing at, this could have spiralled out of control and he obviously did not want that to happen. She had read more into it than was meant and quickly, she pulled herself together, collected her bag and headed for the front door. "Um… it's OK really,

I can see myself out and it's only a hop and skip to my front door, not very far at all. Thank you for a lovely evening."

With that parting shot, she let herself out of his flat and almost ran all the way to her own flat. Letting herself in quickly, she raced into the bedroom and the chaos she had left, threw herself onto her bed and wept her heart out.

Chapter 4
Love

Sleep must have overcome her and on waking, Laura felt absolutely wretched, her head was thumping and her eyes swollen and red. How long she had been there, she did not know but it must have been a long time as her whole body ached. She stretched her arms above her head and moved her fingers which had been scrunched up under her numb face. Reality came back with a rush, and she felt empty and sick.

Humiliation was her uppermost feeling as she was convinced Blair must have thought she was leading him on. He had obviously felt that things had gone a little too far and because of their status gap, and the fact that she was so gauche and naïve, everything had gone wrong.

Laura heaved herself up from the bed and made her way gingerly to the bathroom where she had a shower and emerged some time later, at least feeling a little fresher and ready for a cup of tea. How typical that however bad things got in your life, the first thing you reached for was that revitalising, life-giving cuppa! As she gathered together the makings of her tea and a slice of toast, all the events of the previous evening played through her mind as in slow motion.

How on earth had all this collided; the past coming up to meet the present? As if driven, she knew she had to go back again and her aunt had obviously realised, when she was older, what had happened and the coins were in some sort of date order.

Yes! That had to be it, she was being taken back in precise segments and only by going back and piecing it all together would she unlock the whole story. Aunt Bessy had seen her and she had remembered her.

Laura scrabbled into the living room and unearthed the box of coins. Making sure, once again, she was as far away as possible from her front door, with the added security of the front door key, she took the next bag out and as she turned the coin over in her fingers, noted it was dated 1960.

The ringing in her ears was so high-pitched, it felt as though she had been ejected from a rocket going at warp speed. This time, she seemed to corkscrew in a tumbling, spiralling, twisting motion. Her hair was plastered to her ringing head and a kaleidoscope of colours passed by so quickly, only the shimmer could be seen. This must be what it was like to jump out of a plane and parachute down to the earth. She could feel her face being contorted and could not catch her breath easily, making her feel breathless and alarmed. Suddenly, it all came to an end and all she could hear was a buzzing, screeching noise, when thump... Sprawled on a cold surface, she surveyed the damage she had sustained to her slight frame, checking her arms and legs and looking over her hands, as she rolled over and got herself into an upright position, she could hear raised voices and a young, very angry man in his late teens was standing over... yes...It was Bessy who was holding her hands in front of her, crossed, as if to ward off blows.

"You stupid woman, when will you learn that I have to get hold of more money, I need a fix, I can't wait!" The skinny, scruffy, shaking apology for a human being thrust his contorted face closer to Bessy and shouted,

"Give it to me now or I will beat you senseless, what good are you to me anyway except for the money, hand it over now!"

Aunty Bessie was crying quietly as she handed the young man some notes.

"Please don't do this son, you will end up getting into more trouble."

"Look at you, you are not well and are so thin, please think this through and stop now."

The young man snatched the notes, flicked through the wad and sniffed loudly, saying it would not buy him the 'good stuff' and to save her whining for someone who gave a damn. With that, he stormed out and left, leaving his mother, sobbing uncontrollably. Suddenly, she lifted her head and saw Laura. This time, she did not seem surprised to see her but showed an acceptance of her presence.

"You see what has happened, what is to become of him, I fear for his life!"

Suddenly, the whole room seemed to take on a shimmering quality, and Laura felt a time shift, which caused her to become extremely cold and set her teeth chattering. Laura lost her balance and fell to the floor which was of a liquid substance and she seemed to fall through it, unable to stop herself. Then out of a bright light, she could hear a deep male voice saying, "Don't fret so my dear, he was on a course of self-destruction and had been for a long time now, you tried your best, really, you did but when they are so far gone, nothing will deter them."

"He got hold of a bad fix which just shut him down, he would not have known a thing, he did not come out of the drug-induced coma."

"He was playing with fire and unfortunately got burned and paid the ultimate price. When they get into these drugs, at first it is great and makes them feel good but then the evil takes over and they must have more and more, until they will stop at nothing to obtain it."

"The dealers know this and sell them contaminated fixes for more and more money which is why, like your son, they turn to crime to raise the exorbitant sums the dealers ask. I do not think my dear there would have been any other outcome for your son, I am so sorry."

Then she heard someone crying softly and realised it was Bessie and that her son must have died from his drug taking. How awful, to lose her son and be in such misery. Laura had been concentrating on trying to see through the shimmer and dropped the coin. Immediately, she was transported back, as before, although the vortex that she descended into was like a maelstrom all around her, buffeting her around this way and that and her ears were screeching with pain.

Laura must have blacked out momentarily as she realised she was curled up, with her hands over her ears still, just inside her room. She realised that she too was sobbing and felt all the anguish her aunt had experienced, a hollow vortex occupying her stomach and her mind.

A little later, Laura checked the time and as she guessed, only a few minutes had elapsed. She had to find out more and by her reckoning, there were two more coins in the box. Did she have enough energy to go back again today? She so wanted to but every time she went back, it sapped her strength and left her totally stripped of energy. She would try again in a few days after she had recouped and felt stronger. She did not know if this was actually doing her any harm but she could not get through the vortex and therefore she was not altering any timeline, which she knew was a very dangerous game to play. Unfortunately, she could only watch the past play out and hope that her aunt climbed out of the pit of misery she was stuck in.

Laura went about her business as usual and actively avoided running into Blair.

She left her flat very early and arrived fairly late, always checking to see if his car was there. He had not been home for some time and she remembered him saying he was going away on business for a while. He had tried to ring her the following day, but she had let the answerphone kick-in as she did not feel up to conversing with him just yet.

About a week after all this had happened, Laura was working in the library and categorising some books when she felt someone watching her. As she glanced up, she met with Blair's piercing stare and she could smell his faint clean aftershave. He looked angry and had both hands planted on the counter top, leaning forward urgently.

"So young lady, have you been avoiding me?"

"If not, then you must indeed work very odd, long hours. Also, why have you not returned my calls?"

Laura felt her heart go into overdrive and knew her face was crimson. Mrs Green, who was a regular customer, was looking from one to the other in great expectation that this could be very juicy. Who would have thought that little Laura would have such a handsome, querulous, man-friend. She crossed her arms in front of her body and awaited the response.

"Um, I have been awfully busy and have had to work overtime. I did mean to answer your calls but have been so tired that it went out of my mind, I just seem to have been working and sleeping lately."

Laura did not add that she had thought it best to keep out of his way and that maybe that would suit him better as he had made a big mistake in getting too friendly with her. She also felt bad about the legacy and the coins as he had not known about them, which was odd and possibly upsetting for him. I mean, who was this young girl that Bessy had seen fit to leave a large sum of money and a coin collection? It was all very muddled and awkward and now, here she was, trapped at work with Mrs Green awaiting the outcome and possibly half the library listening in!

"Ah-ha! I thought as much, you are too pale, and I am sure you have lost weight, you are working far too hard."

Blair leaned in closer, giving the ladies both side of him a wink, before turning his attention to Laura, who by now, looked like a rabbit caught in a car's headlights and not able to move a muscle.

"I wanted to get together with you again to discuss matters and wondered if you would come out with me to a restaurant, of your choosing, so that we can talk? No pressure, somewhere popular, just a discussion."

"What do you say?"

Laura was aware of Mrs Green and by now, a half dozen people standing by the counter were awaiting her answer. They all had their heads turned in her direction, heads cocked to one side, in anticipation. Laura felt trapped as this was so public and they were all waiting for her to answer. Mrs Green coughed and said, "Go on Laura say yes, he seems like a very nice gentleman."

This had Laura blushing again and to get everyone off her back, she glanced at him under her long sweeping lashes and uttered softly, "Ok!"

Blair visibly relaxed and named a local restaurant in the high street which was very popular and had a good reputation.

"I will pick you up at 7:30 tonight, see you then."

With that, he turned on his heel and made a very quick exit, but not before he gave all the ladies a huge grin, and left Laura totally unable to even take a breath. Well, of all the high-handed cheek! Suddenly, a little cheer went up from the customers gathered around her and they all started clapping.

"It brings a tear to my eye," said Mrs Green and gave Laura's hand a quick squeeze as she made her way out. The rest of the day passed in a complete haze.

That night she flew home and had a quick shower, washing her hair at the same time. Hurrying into her bedroom, she threw open her wardrobe doors and inspected the array of items hanging therein. "A rather motley crew," she said to herself as she frantically rifled through the hangers, discarding one after another. As luck would have it, a rather lovely dress caught her eye that she had purchased a couple of months ago, on a complete whim. It was in a half-price sale and because it was her favourite shade of coral, merited a second glance. It was fairly figure hugging, but in a good way, with an all over floral theme on a cream background. She quickly tried it on, teaming it with neutral sandals, a beautiful satin coral clutch and a little coral shrug. She twirled this way and that in front of the full-length mirror on the back of the wardrobe door. Her hair was shoulder length and so glossy that it looked like spun silk.

She gave a sort of nod of approval to herself and exited the bedroom to emerge into the hallway, flustered but pleased with her ensemble for the evening. True to his word, Blair was waiting downstairs by the car and his eyes lit up at her approach.

"A very good evening to you Laura and may I say, you look utterly charming tonight, your carriage awaits."

Laura beamed up at him and gave a small nod as she got into the front seat. Blair made sure her dress was not caught in the door and slammed it shut before going round to the driver's seat. He got in swiftly and gunned the engine, drawing away smoothly from the entrance. Once he had manoeuvred the car out into the night traffic, he gave her an appraising glance.

"I hope you are hungry because I sure am, I have been travelling all day and missed lunch."

Laura was dismayed and said, "Oh dear, I suppose it goes with your job that you frequently miss meals in order to meet deadlines with your work."

"I am afraid so as sometimes, I have connections to make and just can't spare the time."

"However, enough about me and more about you!"

"I want to know if you have been avoiding me and if so, why?"

"I really did not mean to frighten you off the other night but thought that I had overstepped the mark, so to speak."

Laura kept her eyes on her hands which were clasped tightly in her lap and then made a small sigh.

"Honestly Blair, it is me who should be apologising to you as I should not have left in such a hurry, but I feel I don't really fit into your lifestyle and I thought you were just being polite!"

Blair was drawing up outside the restaurant and he slowly killed the engine and turned to face her, his face in half shadow.

"Don't ever think that Laura, yes, I move in fairly high business circles but it does not mean I have to enjoy it."

I am a fairly uncomplicated man and have really good friends who I have known since school and some are struggling to make their way in this tough world we live in.

We do not measure our friendship in cash or status, we are friends and it is not complicated. Blair leaned forwards, his elbows resting on the table and his hands making a pyramid under his chin.

"Am I making a hash of this and sounding pompous?"

It was his turn to look down at his hands and wait for her answer. Laura turned to him and laid her hand on his arm.

"I think you have explained things very well and I understand what you are trying to convey. Let's start again with no false ideas of each other and enjoy our meal." Blair looked pleased and offered her his hand which she promptly shook.

They entered the restaurant and were shown a secluded table for two, off to the side of the main hub of tables. For the first half an hour, they chose their meals and drinks and exchanged small talk. The first course was delivered and promptly demolished by both parties, ready for their mains. Blair had chosen a rump steak with all the trimmings and Laura, chicken wrapped in Parma ham and served with a delicious mushroom sauce, dauphinois potatoes and mixed vegetables. The smell was amazing and they both smiled at each other across the table before savouring their meals with small interjections of *ummm* and *ahh*. Whilst they waited for their desserts, they talked about the day and various trivialities. However, Blair could not take his eyes from her face and did not hear the waitress approach for their dishes.

"Is everything to your liking sir?" the waitress enquired, smiling at them both.

Blair reluctantly took his gaze away from Laura and smiled and nodded in affirmative, words not on hand immediately.

"Is there anything else I can get you, maybe a coffee or a liqueur to compliment your meal?"

"Yes, a coffee would be good, are you OK with that Laura?"

She had been in a trance-like state and just nodded and smiled her approval, not taking her eyes from his face. They finished their desserts and the waitress brought the aromatic coffee, pouring it into little gold cups, leaving them to add cream if they wished. Laura had a dash of cream in hers, but Blair liked his coffee as it came. They did not speak, just eye contact, whilst they slowly sipped their coffee.

It was a pleasurable silence and the air was electric and alive with unspoken endearments.

Blair settled the bill and left a generous tip for the beaming girl who had served them.

She watched them exit the restaurant and sighed audibly. Her friend who was passing with a huge pile of plates heard it and lifted an eyebrow in question.

"Such a lovely couple and so in love, it almost makes up for the crazy mixed up world we live in and gives us all hope."

The other girl nodded and smiled her understanding as working in catering really was hard and unrewarding, the pay minimal. If one couple made it, then maybe it was all worth it, just maybe…

Blair took Laura home and saw her to the door of her flat. He took her by the shoulders, oh so gently and pulled her to him, wrapping his long, strong arms completely around her small frame. As before, for a while, he just held her tight, revelling in the wonderful feeling it gave him to just capture her, inhale her sweet perfume and relish in her soft, compliant curves. He then tipped her chin towards him and with a lift of his elegant eyebrow, he gently covered her waiting lips. He deepened the kiss and nuzzled her soft, swollen lips open. He let his tongue play around her lips before entering her beautiful mouth and feeling the moist sweetness waiting for him. Laura was just lost. She had never felt this way about anyone and the electric pulses generated from his touch were threatening to engulf her. She wanted more and pressed herself closer to his strong, muscled torso. His hand cupped her face and splayed around her cheek to gently touch her earlobe, trailing down to her neck, which she so elegantly displayed for him. Blair pulled away gently and stared down at her for what seemed like aeons of time.

Laura was dizzy and swayed slightly at which point, Blair caught her up in his strong arms, took the key she miraculously still had in her hand, opened the door of the flat and stepped in. Once inside, he closed the door with a back-kick of his foot and took her through to the lounge where he carefully laid her down.

"I can't get enough of you, your sweetness overwhelms me, intoxicates me; I am lost my pretty one, totally and utterly lost."

Blair lowered his tall, muscular frame gently down onto her fragile, beautiful body. He held himself slightly away from crushing her completely with his outstretched arms on each side of her tousled head. From this vantage point, he could observe her huge, long-lashed eyes staring up at him. See the flush of heat across her cheekbones and the way she was barely breathing in anticipation of his next move. He lowered himself gently towards her right ear and whispered oh, so, slowly, "Are you OK with this Laura, as this really is the point of no return?"

Laura sighed, a deep contented sigh, and threw her arms around his neck, whispering in his ear in turn, "Oh Blair, I so am!"

As if an orchestra had begun to play, they moved in perfect harmony, Blair was kissing her so softly with myriad, feather-soft butterfly kisses from her eyes, down her cheek, deftly missing her eager mouth and continuing on to her neck and dealing with the problem of her clothing, as if she had none. It was all done in one fluid movement until Laura felt the heat of his bare flesh against hers and she immediately went up in flames, consumed by a white-hot caldron of passion that left her breathless but eager, panting, wanting, needing to feel him inside her. Laura arched her back and pulled him closer until she tensed with a pain so fleeting, it was gone almost before it had begun.

Blair felt her tense and would have pulled back, but Laura firmly urged him on making little mews of pleasure as he, gently at first, slowly slid inside her sheath of silk. He gradually increased the pace and Laura abandoned her very being to him at this moment in time. Like molten lava, something inside of her was bubbling to the surface, taking her higher than she had ever known and all too soon, she reached the molten peak and it was as if her whole being was aflame and fizzing upwards towards her sweet climax. Blair tried to hold back but he could not as he heard her call out, causing him to explode so fiercely and with such intensity that he also called out, wrapping her to himself tightly, until his spasms eased and his breathing returned to some normality. They lay there, molten hot, slicked with moisture, and both panting slightly as if they had run a marathon. Blair spoke first, his voice cracked with emotion.

"Laura, that was the most gorgeous experience of my life, I just want to reassure you that I did take precautions, although how I did it in time, I shall never know."

"I hope I did not hurt you as I guess it was your first time?"

Laura opened her eyes slowly, stretched her whole body like a cat, gave him a huge grin and pulled him close.

"You were amazingly gentle Blair, and I adored it and you."

"However, I am beautifully tired now."

"Are you going to stay with me?"

In answer to her query, Blair kissed her gently and held her tight in his strong arms. "Just try and stop me," he murmured.

Where do you go from here? Laura was completely and utterly in love with Blair but she felt he was too sophisticated for her and she was just a little light relief in his busy complicated life. Blair's world was totally different to hers and she did not think people who moved in those high circles actually committed to anyone or anything! She had been a fool yesterday and gone with her heart but now feared it could be broken into jagged pieces of ice!

Blair had stayed until early and then had quietly left, whilst she was deeply sleeping, leaving her a note to say he had early business meetings and would see her that night, although, it could be late. On waking, she had read the note and all the doubts had begun to creep in as to why he would want a nobody like her. The old self-doubting, shy Laura surfaced and obliterated the wonderful evening she had experienced, the ragged emotions she had felt and the love she held for him, forever locked away in her naive, young, gullible heart. Suddenly, she remembered the coins. She must go back to find out how Bessie had met Blair's father and what had happened and resolved to do it that morning!

Chapter 5
Happiness

After showering and finding she was stiff and achy from her unfamiliar exertions the night before, she positioned herself, as before, the farthest place away from the door and opened the box. Of course, there were many other coins and collections contained therein but only the one in the velvet pouch, which had so intrigued her. Carefully, she delved into the pouch and pulled out the fifth coin, quickly turning it to see the date – 1965. However, this time she felt more pressure on her whole being and put her hands to her ears, mindful of the coin, to try and stop the pain, as air seemed to rush by her and fill her head. This was getting more dangerous, she realised, and let herself be carried along in the vortex the coin had created. Her whole body trembled and shook and she was spinning out of control. Not for the first time, Laura was actually physically scared and wondered if she would make her way back to her time zone without harm.

Uhh… As before, she seemed to slide along an imaginary chute and this time, she actually tried to go with it and crossed her arms over the front of her body so that she did not twist and turn so much. Whether it was this action or not but the journey did not seem to take so long and… ***Smack!*** she was deposited, none too gently, on the floor of what looked like a jewellery shop. She looked all around her and yes, there were glass cabinets full of sparkling gems: rings, necklaces, bracelets and earrings.

In one cabinet was silverware, the likes she had never seen, and another seemed to hold, was she right, a collection of coins! Laura started to get her hearing back, although her ears throbbed with pain and she could now see a man and woman behind the counter, talking to a young woman who was in the shop, presumably a customer.

"Yes, my dear," said Bessy.

Yes, it was her, but an elegant, beautifully dressed Bessy. My word, what had happened in the intervening years? Whatever it was must have worked a miracle because Bessy had undergone a complete transformation.

"That could be done in a jiffy if you leave the bracelet with me, I will see that a new catch is put on with a safety chain, giving you more security.

"You are very lucky you felt it slip from your wrist and managed to catch it.

"It will be ready in a day or two for you to pick up," Bessy smiled at her customer, a lovely, confident smile and bid her farewell and a good morning. As she stepped back slightly, Laura caught her eye and at first, she must have thought she was another customer but then recognition took hold and she actually beamed at Laura and clasped her hands together, almost jumping up and down with delight.

"It's you, isn't it? I can see you more clearly, I know it is you."

"Can we possibly go to a nearby tea shop, where I can tell you what has happened to me since you last visited?"

Laura did not know if this was possible but as Bessy had remarked, she seemed able to see her more clearly this time and, careful not to get too close, followed Bessy across the road to the little tea shop.

They sat down opposite each other, although Laura found as last time, she was just hovering over her chair and would obviously not be able to drink the tea when it came.

Bessy looked amazing and so happy. Not waiting for the tea to arrive, she looked at Laura intently and smiled broadly.

"I am so glad you have come as I have found the most wonderful man who loves me and cares for me."

"He has a young son called Blair and he is a dear child, so good-natured and already good looking although still young."

"He can charm the birds from the trees and does so well at school, I would think he will be a great success when he is older."

The tea arrived and Bessy poured the steaming liquid into two cups, adding milk.

Laura did not have the heart to explain that she would not be able to join her, when Bessy continued, "I met my husband when I worked in that awful fish shop, he used to come in and buy fish regularly for himself and his son.

"One day, I was so upset and as I had not completed a task on time and had been threatened with the sack and had nowhere to live.

"It was a regular tactic used against me but, sometimes, the untenable position in which I had found myself came crashing down around me and I could see no future. Bessy shrugged her slim shoulders and turned her hands palm upwards, shaking her elegant head.

"I began to cry whilst serving him and he comforted me and took me to this very tea shop where I told him of my horrible existence and he was so kind and gentle, putting an arm around my shoulders and letting me cry.

"He offered me a job in his jewellers and said he could find lodgings for me nearby. I knew he was a good man and took him at his word, leaving that night, for good or ill, I knew not which. Bessy smiled broadly her beautiful eyes sparkling brightly like diamonds.

"It was all good and not long before I knew, he was the one for me and we were married within a year.

"I have rebuilt my life with his loving kindness and have not looked back."

Laura smiled at her and felt her heart swell with emotion. How wonderful that Aunt Bessie had found happiness and rebuilt her life after such tragedy and bitterness.

They walked back to the jewellery shop, talking as they went.

"Oh Bessie, I am so thrilled for you and glad I have made the journey back again, although I fear I may not be able to return as it gets more dangerous each time I travel, it worries me that I will not be able to visit you again and will be caught in between our worlds in time and space.

"This proves that time travel is possible, I don't know how, why or what triggers it but I know I have experienced something of a magnitude greater than anyone could imagine.

"The forces that are at work here are beyond comprehension.

"I wish I had more time with you but am so glad you are now safe and cared for."

"I will remember you my dear," Bessie said and her voice was becoming very faint and the air all around her started to shimmer and Laura felt herself shudder and shake until her teeth chattered and she could feel the overwhelming pressure again. The coin dropped from her nerveless fingers before she could stop it and as she looked up, Bessie was enveloped in a haze of light, sparkling as on water.

Laura reached out her hand as if to stop herself from leaving and called out to Bessie, "It will be alright you know, all will be well and you will have a wonderful life." Laura did not know if Bessie heard her as she was carried along in prisms of light and shaken by forces beyond her comprehension. This was not good. It felt different and it was as if she were in an imaginary cage, being held against her will. Try as she might, she could not seem to escape and the noise was deafening and so scary, she could feel her heart beating loudly above it all, what had she done? She hadn't tampered with anything that she knew of, or had she? Had she accidentally touched Bessie whilst in the shop and would that mean time zones had been shifted, even if only by milliseconds? If only she had been more careful not to alter anything, this did not feel right.

She felt so cold, icy and she was constricted now, she could not move her limbs and they felt like lead. Everything was passing by her at such speed and she could hear voices breaking through the incredible noise. Like shifting sand, she had no substance and was spiralling down in a kaleidoscope of colour and light. Oh dear, what was happening, she must get back, she must.

Chapter 6
Bessy's Story

On returning to the shop, Bessy stood for a long time, looking at the place where Laura had appeared, in deep contemplation of the unusual visits she had received from Laura over the years. This was not the first time she had thought about it but there had never been time to really question the situation before.

Bessy looked around as if for inspiration, and her eyes dropped to the large cabinet containing the coin collections to her left. Slowly, she walked towards it as if drawn by a magnet and came to stand in front of the large glass display. Immediately, she picked out several coins along the front which somehow had an iridescent glow to them. When she peered into the display she discovered they were in date order 1927, 1943, 1955, 1960 and 1965 (this year)! Bessy quickly went behind the cabinet and unlocked the sliding door with a key from the many she had on a keychain kept in her pocket.

She pulled out the tray containing the coins and placed it on the top of the counter and stared. Sure enough, the dates coincided with Laura's visits and when she picked the first one up, an electric energy was transmitted to her whole hand and arm, causing her to drop the coin at first.

Could she, in some unfathomable way, use these coins to bring Laura back in time to see her life? Was there some underlying reason as to why she was able to come back and would they be reunited in the future?

Laura seemed such a lovely girl and so pretty and truly wanted to help Bessy but had been unable to do so because of the time shift. It would be fantastic if perhaps, depending on when she was born, she could meet up with her stepson in the future when, who knows, they could meet and perhaps, just perhaps, fall in love. Once this thought was conceived, Bessy could not let it go and popped the coins into little velvet pouches, then into her pocket to think what she could do with them. Her husband had gone out to see a buyer and would be some time and the shop was not very busy this afternoon, so she went through to the little room in the back to make another cup of tea whilst she contemplated what to do next.

It was really a fragmented thought forming as to how she was going to get the coins to Laura but she realised that she was going to do it as she was sure that is what brought Laura back again and again. There must be some sort of force contained within the coins that enabled time travel, she did not really dwell on the reasons of why's or wherefores as to where this great force could have originated but was absolutely certain that it was possible. She was also convinced that there was a purpose to it and that could very well be connected in the future. Whilst Bessy sat at the table, she deposited the coins in a row in front of her and spanning them all, laid her hands on them.

Immediately, the coins began to glow and agitate under her hands, she felt an icy cold blast fill the room and it became as dark as night. Somehow, she found she could not remove her hands from the coins and the glow created by them was increasing until she was almost at one with them.

It was as if the room had been separated from the shop and she was sitting high in the air looking down at herself (if that were possible), there was a deafening noise beginning to erupt all around her and the glow became an outline of something which she could not quite make out.

Bessy did not feel frightened by what was happening and stayed quite calm, the reason for which, she could not comprehend but just knew this was not life-threatening. There seemed to be images appearing in front of her and yes, it was Laura, she was sure of it, sitting at a desk of some sort. Then a man appeared in front of her and began talking but she could not make out any words but he looked familiar. Could it be…? Was it…? Yes, it was Blair, her stepson, grown into a very handsome man and he was deep in conversation with Laura. The images were very watery and indistinct and faded into another image in which Laura was holding out her hand as if asking Bessy to help her. Then just as suddenly, the images disappeared and Bessy felt herself descending slowly back into the shop just as she had been, sitting at the desk, the tea still steaming, the coins back in their pouches now!

Bessy felt as though she had been drained of her life force and her whole body felt incredibly tired. It was a good job she had made a cup of tea as she really needed it at this precise time and also to try and make some sense of the incident. The whole episode had only taken minutes and now it seemed so unreal, but Bessy was determined to formulate a plan that would start the chain reaction.

She had the coins and would bide her time but knew in her heart that at some time in the future, she would get the opportunity to deliver the coins to Laura. Just then, the shop doorbell rang and Bessy drained her tea cup, setting it down gently on the table, gave a pat to her hair, composed herself and made her way into the shop, putting to one side for the moment the mystery she had to solve.

Time passed and it was 1971, the years had been good to Bessy and her life could not have been better. She adored her husband and of course her stepson, who in turn loved her dearly. Her husband came through from the back room and smiled before bending to kiss her lightly on her cheek.

"Hello, my dear, have you had a good morning with your lady friends?"

He went to put the kettle on and asked if she would like a cup of coffee to which she said she would and he carried on, "I took a phone message for you from your niece and she has had a baby girl, all is well and her name is Laura."

Robert did not see his wife's reaction to this news and carried on, "I know you don't really have much to do with your first husband's family, but it was kind of them to let us know, don't you think?"

Bessy could only nod as her mind was in a whirl at this utterly incredulous news, it had happened, Laura had been born, just as she thought, and so her plan could now be put into action. She would send a card and a gift and hopefully get to meet her soon, although they lived a long way from her niece, who had always been very distant and unfriendly, not wanting to keep in contact with her over the years. Yes, it would be difficult, but she was sure that a meeting in the future should be possible.

"How lovely Robert, wonderful news, although, I am surprised they let us know, we must try to visit them if they will let us."

Bessy tried several times in the next few years to see Laura but was always put off by her mother, who was always making excuses as to why they could not visit. However, eventually, when Laura was about three years old, they had a meeting and Bessy took her box of coins. She showed them to the little girl, carefully making sure she wore thick gloves when handling them, in order not to activate their energy.

Laura was so pretty and interested in all Bessy told her, although too young to really understand. It became clear to Bessy that she could not give the coins to Laura until she was older, and one huge reason was her mother! Laura's mother was openly hostile to Bessy, the reason not being clear, but probably because she was just wired that way. If Bessy gave Laura the coins now, she was sure her mother would take them and sell them for whatever she could get, it was obvious that she chased a finer life for herself and would do anything to achieve it. This was a complication that she had not foreseen and, therefore, because of the unwillingness for Robert and herself to visit, she would have to overcome.

When Robert died, it was utterly devastating for Bessie, he was her world and she realised that it was the end of an era for her. Blair had long since left home and was a successful businessman who travelled the world. He kept in touch and came to see her as often as he could but her zest for life had waned with Robert's passing. She moved out of the big house they had together and chose a lovely bungalow in an elderly complex, which gave her help and companionship. Bessy was not in good health and knew time was not on her side, but no matter, as her beloved Robert had gone. Her goal of getting the coins to Laura had not been forgotten and had been dealt with a few years previously. She knew in her heart all would be well and go to plan as it was meant to be.

Bessy was not unhappy as she had such wonderful memories, more than most achieved during their lifetimes. Now she was content as she was certain the forces beyond her comprehension would begin and, maybe, a little magic might happen.

Chapter 7
Blair

Blair had been to two meetings and they had been so boring, he would have loved to just walk out but they were crucial to his business. All he could think about was Laura and her lovely face and silky body against his. He could not wait to get back to her and declare his love, yes, that was what he felt and it had taken him a long time to finally find someone who he adored and wanted to make a life with. Laura had got under his skin and in his head. As soon as he was able to, he excused himself from the after-meeting drinks and chat, located his car and speedily made his way home. He could not concentrate and possibly jumped a light at a small junction.

As Blair was going back to see Laura at the flat, he began reflecting on his life and what it meant to him. His relationship with Bessy had been really good and he knew she was his step-mother, but it had never really felt like that at all. Since he was really young, she had looked after him and had always given him her time and love. His father had cared for her deeply and their family unit had been tight. He had been encouraged to go to university and had really enjoyed his time there and of course, that is where he had learnt his business skills. He had graduated and got a job with a good financial firm and started completely at the bottom of the pile. He had been a gopher and was at the beck and call of several high-powered, successful people. He had earned their respect and climbed the ladder quite quickly with their help and support. He now ran his own business and was really successful and well respected in the higher circles. Blair never backed down from a challenge and always did his business by the book. This did not always bring him instant success but in the long run, he found that by being honest and above board, clients would come back to him and they would seek him out, knowing he would not let them down. He had dated a lot over the years and at one time had a long-term relationship with a very lovely woman whom he thought would be the one he would settle down with but, alas, it was not to be as she fell in love with his best friend and they were now married with two little children. Thinking about it, he really did not think he loved her enough as it did not really devastate him and he was still friends with them both, if at a distance. However, Laura was another matter and he could not get her out of his head. Technically, she was not a beauty but when she smiled her face lit up and her eyes sparkled with mischief, one eyebrow arching up as if to challenge him. She was really petite and looked so fragile, but it was a complete smokescreen as she was entirely independent and had been so for a long while. Since the night with her in the flat, he was totally hooked and knew he was going to ask her to marry him as soon possible. There was no need to wait as he knew his own mind and was sure she felt the same way. He also saw it as a sign that she had known Bessy, who had left her a small legacy. It was surely a signal that their paths were meant to cross at some time and he was positive she was the one for him and secretly he was sure that Bessy knew it also. It was all very strange and if he really thought about it, pretty damn spooky really but not in a bad way, just in a really, really good way.

Finally he pulled up in the drive, leapt from the car and made his way straight to Laura's flat, taking the stairs two at a time.

Once there, he knocked on the door and stood back against the wall, waiting for Laura to appear, but she didn't open the door so he rapped on it again and listened. There seemed to be something happening inside the flat as he could see lights flickering under the door, also, he thought he could hear a noise like that of howling wind. What in the name of all that is holy was going on?

"Laura! Are you in there?"

No reply, just the noise getting louder, and the door began to shake.

"Laura?"

Blake put his ear to the door to see if he could hear her.

"Answer me for pity's sake."

Blair could take no more and put his shoulder against the door, it did not budge. Keys. Were they in his pocket? He felt frantically in his suit and looked in his bag but no keys. Stupid man, he had left them on his hall table this morning in his haste to exit his flat. Blair flew down the stairs, gained entry to his flat, snatched up the keys and once again ascended the stairs at a frantic pace.

His hand shook as he put the key in the lock and he felt physically sick at what he might find when he entered.

As Blair threw open the door, several things became apparent. One was Laura sprawled on the floor of her flat, her hair splayed out around her. The utter raw cold inside the flat had him shivering immediately and the pungent smell that met his nostrils causing him to cough violently in protest. He immediately bent down to Laura and checked her breathing and pulse. Her breath was shallow and her pulse weak. She was a block of ice and her hands had a blue tinge. He caught her up gently and began to rub her arms and cradle her to the warmth of his body to transfer some heat between them.

"Oh my darling, what on God's earth has happened to you?"

He sat with her cradled in his arms for what seemed a lifetime, until suddenly, she gave a small moan and moved her head from side to side as if to ward off pain.

"My darling, speak to me, what has happened?"

There was no response and Laura's pallor was ashen.

"I have called an ambulance for you, don't worry help is on the way my love, just hang on and fight."

Blair wrapped his strong arms even more tightly around her, willing some of his strength into her limp, frozen body. What on earth had happened? When he left this morning, she was fine. He could hear the faint wail of a siren in the distance and hoped it would arrive quickly before he lost her.

Chapter 8
Future Beginnings

Lights, bright lights, uhh… My head hurts, so where am I? Laura became aware that she was moving through a brightly-lit corridor. There seemed to be a lot of confusion and noise all around her until she entered a large room with lots of apparatus on the walls and huge ceiling lights. At this point, she realised it must be a hospital room. What had she done? Why couldn't she remember? Her brain was not functioning properly and had cotton wool inside. Everything was muffled, it was like being underwater but not!

"Hurry, her stats are falling and her temperature needs to be increased or we will lose her," said a female voice sharply. Laura felt a scratch on her arm where they were attaching a drip and she was connected up to a bank of machines which would help them monitor her vital signs. Confusion reigned and she felt herself being wrapped in a foil-like substance. Oh she was cold, so cold.

"Laura can you hear me?"

Blair bent over her still, fragile body and whispered into her pretty ear,

"Come on darling, hang on in there, fight, and breathe."

A male voice was urging her to fight her way back to consciousness. Oh my, but it was a huge ask. It was so easy to give in to the cold and drift away on a feather-like cloud of deep sleep.

Laura could hear whispering, chattering noises as if a radio was on search mode and could not quite locate the right one. Gradually, she began to make out odd words and she turned her head to one side to better hear the disjointed conversation that was going on around her.

"Look, she is moving her head, and I am sure I saw her eyes flicker."

"Laura! Laura! Can you hear us?"

"Squeeze my hand if you can, my darling," said a deep, familiar voice. Laura slowly opened her beautiful eyes which felt glued together with huge weights pressing down on them. It took such an effort to raise her consciousness and try to focus.

There were several people round her and her hand was covered in a large firm grasp, the thumb stroking her fingers gently.

"Blair?" Laura felt disorientated and mumbled, "Is that you?"

"I mean really and truly you?" Blair smiled broadly, taking in a deep calming breath and answered,

"Yes, my love, it is really and truly me and I am here for you always."

"You have given us such a fright, we thought we had lost you."

Blair's usually strong, deep voice broke on the words and he lifted her hand to his lips and kissed her fingers gently.

"Oh Blair, I thought I had lost me too and I would never get back to you."

Laura started to sob gently, the tears flowing down her lovely face.

"Hush little one, try to get some sleep and we will talk more when you are less exhausted."

Laura then drifted off into a more normal sleep she so desperately needed and all in the room breathed sighs of relief, as it was now a matter of her gaining strength, she was out of the woods.

Blair had been questioned by the police who had also been called to the flat. They had searched the premises thoroughly and could find no trace of a forced entry, other than Blair's attempt to gain access to the flat to get to Laura. There was nothing taken, nothing moved and no sign of a struggle.

Because of the cold Blair felt on entering the flat and the pungent smell, it was checked over for any gas leak or electric failure of some kind but all was correct and working. The authorities were stumped and could find no reason for Laura's collapse.

Blair sat vigilant all night, his own sleep and comfort of no importance. How had he let this petite, young woman get in under the iron radar that he had built around himself for so long? What in heaven's name had happened to her in the flat to nearly take her life? Only she could tell him if she could remember and with that thought, he too, drifted into an uneasy slumber filled with fearful dreams of what might have happened had he not been there.

The soft morning fingers of light were beginning to fill the room and Laura had been awake for a little while now, gathering her senses and piecing all the fragments of the last 24 hours together. She should never had gone back that last time as she knew it was getting dangerous but did not realise just how life-threatening it was going to be.

Blair was here and he had found her. What must he have thought? She glanced over to where he was asleep in the high-backed chair, even in sleep he looked so handsome.

Her whole body ached so deeply to her very core. That was indeed some journey back this time. There was now no need to visit the past again even though one coin still remained, because she was looking at her future!

It had all been mapped out for her in some master plan that she had no control over. Do any of us get to see into the past to connect with our future as she had done? Aunt Bessemer had remembered her visit and set the wheels in motion, although how she had achieved it Laura would never know. Did her Aunt have some gift so powerful that she could transfer it to the set of coins, wishing and hoping her little scheme for the two of them to meet and perhaps, just perhaps, fall in love. It was well known that some people were receivers and some transmitters, and she and her Aunt must be opposites, enabling Laura to go back in time and connect with the past.

"Well Bessy, I think you did it." Laura looked heavenward.

There is more in heaven and earth than we know or can comprehend but you and I have been a part of something that neither of us can explain.

It may be that we saw something that happens all the time but we are all too busy with our lives to see it.

Does the past exist parallel to our world?

Have I crossed dimensions to be able to find my future happiness? Laura looked across to where Blaire was sleeping, utterly exhausted.

When Blaire awakens, I will try and explain but I must be aware that he may be unable to take it all in and think I have a concussion from the incident in the flat. No matter, I think he will eventually realise that we were meant to meet, past, future or present. This was preordained, our destiny, our time to Live, Love and be Happy. Laura had been able to

GO BACK FOR LOVE

Epilogue

Eventually, Laura slipped into a deep slumber, no longer in danger, with Blair sleeping only feet away from her. What they both did not see and realise was the old lady who entered the hospital room, gently gliding through the closed door. She came to rest by the bed and looked from one to the other, a serene smile on her lovely face. The lines of age had disappeared, and Bessy was young and beautiful, by her side, her darling husband had materialised and he encircled her slight body with his steady arm, squeezing her shoulders lovingly.

"I don't know how you did it Bess my darling, but you have pulled off a miracle."

Bessy looked up at her husband and smiled.

"It is no miracle, my darling, it is the circle of life, and if you listen and believe, you can do anything. There are no barriers, no time zones, only faith and love."

Do you believe you can…

GO BACK FOR LOVE